Wings of Light

The Migration of the Yellow Butterfly

Stephen R. Swinburne

Illustrated by Bruce Hiscock

Boyds Mills Press

Grateful thanks to Thomas C. Emmel, Ph.D., director, McGuire Center for Lepidoptera and Biodiversity, Florida Museum of Natural History; Lincoln Brower, Ph.D., research professor of biology, Sweet Briar College and Distinguished Service Professor of Zoology, Emeritus, University of Florida; Adam Porter, Ph.D., Department of Plant, Soil, and Insect Sciences & Graduate Program in Organismic and Evolutionary Biology, University of Massachusetts; and Ms. Audrey Grabowski

Published by Boyds Mills Press, Inc.
A Highlights Company
815 Church Street
Honesdale, Pennsylvania 18431
Printed in China

Library of Congress Cataloging-in-Publication Data

Swinburne, Stephen R.
Wings of light : a migration of butterflies from the rain forest to your backyard / by Stephen R. Swinburne ; illustrated by Bruce Hiscock.— 1st ed.
p. cm.
ISBN 1-59078-082-5 (alk. paper)
1. Butterflies—Migration—Juvenile literature. I. Hiscock, Bruce. II. Title.

QL544.2.S95 2006
595.78'91568—dc22   2005021140

First edition, 2006
The text of this book is set in 14-point Minion.
The illustrations are done in watercolor.

10 9 8 7 6 5 4 3 2 1

To the staff of Boyds Mills Press, steadfast and true
—S. R. S.

With love to my mother, Clara, my unfailing source of encouragement
—B. H.

IT IS A SUMMER MORNING on the rain forest floor in the Yucatan Peninsula. A yellow butterfly with a notch in its wing, sliced by a bird's beak, flutters across the sunbeams. The butterfly spirals upward and weaves around moss and orchid-covered branches.

A lizard, hidden along a nearby limb, darts out. The butterfly dodges and flies up through the canopy. For an instant, it hovers over a sea of green trees, sensing the direction to go. The butterfly veers away, flying with strong, steady wingbeats in a direct path, northeast.

The butterfly with a notch in its wing is joined by another. The sun warms them. Soon the two insects are joined by others, as if some quiet signal has passed through the forest. Within an hour, hundreds and hundreds of butterflies beat their pale yellow wings above the forests of the Yucatan Peninsula and fly toward the sea.

By midafternoon, the migration of yellow butterflies has grown to thousands. They drift like a slow-moving cloud above the canopy. The butterflies approach the coast and feel the strong ocean breeze buffeting their wings. They settle in the trees. Many of them fly to feed on the forest flowers. As the sun falls, thousands of butterflies fold their wings and sleep, huddled among the silent trees. The butterfly with a notch in its wing perches on a bromeliad living on the branch of a fig tree.

The next morning, the forest, from mossy floor to canopy, moves in flashes of yellow wings. The sun heats the air as warm as a greenhouse. The butterflies rise to the canopy. They leave the trees in steady streams and fly up into brilliant sunshine. The butterfly with a notch in its wing senses a day of light winds and warm temperatures. The swarm of butterflies wings over the Gulf of Mexico northeast to the mainland of North America.

The butterflies move in a long, wavering line high above the ocean waves. The butterflies fly fast and strong. Their wing muscles are nourished by the sugars of tropical flowers. The winds rise out of the south, propelling the butterflies.

Far out to sea, some of the yellow butterflies tire and lose speed. A few flutter too close to the ocean and are dashed by the waves. Luckier ones find rest on a slow-moving freighter crossing the path of the butterfly migration. They alight on the ship's railings and decks and bask on the wide containers of freight. The butterfly with a notch in its wing is a strong flyer. He and thousands of others beat their wings tirelessly. They fly mile after mile through the bright light above the Gulf of Mexico.

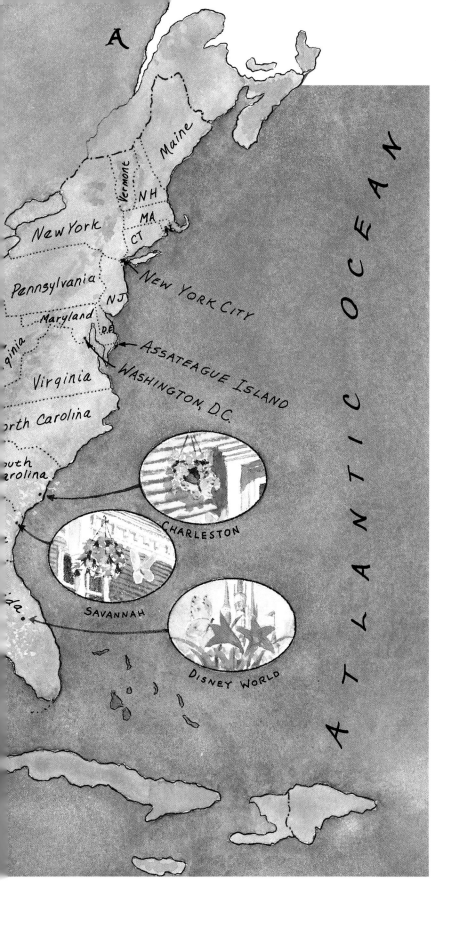

Southerly winds push the butterflies on and on. Stretched out hundreds of miles wide, the cloud of butterflies reach land. They advance across the cattle country and citrus groves of central Florida, over the swamps of Louisiana, into the southern states of Georgia, Alabama, and Texas.

Once the migration reaches land, a steady stream of butterflies peels away from the main flight. They disperse over the countryside to feed and rest and mate. The yellow butterflies drink the nectar of sidewalk flowers in New Orleans, Louisiana; dash among the display gardens in the Magic Kingdom of Disney World; feed in the hanging flower baskets of Savannah, Georgia, and Charleston, South Carolina. Fanning out in a broad front, the migration of yellow butterflies scatters across the southern United States.

The butterfly with a notch in its wing moves steadily northward with hundreds of others. The eastern tip of the butterfly flight passes over herds of wild ponies on Assateague Island, Maryland. The western edge of butterflies sails pass the promenades and memorials of Washington, D.C.

Thirty-five days after leaving the rain forest of the Yucatan Peninsula, the butterfly with a notch in its wing seeks shelter in an oak tree in New York City's Central Park. Rain pelts the buildings and parks. All two hundred migrating yellow butterflies close their wings and wait out the storm.

The next day, on a warm afternoon, the butterfly with a notch in its wing arrives in southern Vermont. In a wide, backyard garden, the yellow butterfly hovers above the wet nose of a golden retriever sleeping in the sun. The dog yawns and chases it, but the butterfly flies off to join other yellow butterflies at the other end of the garden.

In the background, male and female yellow butterflies feed on flower nectar and bask in the sunshine. The yellow butterflies rest with closed wings. They turn sideways to the sun. The butterfly with a notch in its wing searches for a mate. He wings close to a female, but she spirals upward, avoiding him. He gives up and drops quickly to the garden to find another female.

He sees a female perched on a red zinnia. He flutters above her, as delicately as a feather held by the wind. He lightly touches her with his legs and wings. She trembles in response. He lands beside her and they mate.

Over the next two days, the female lays many eggs on the underside of a cassia plant in a nearby vegetable patch. One hot summer morning, the butterfly with a notch in its wing flies feebly away from the backyard flower garden. The sun is strong but the butterfly sails low to the ground, its wings tattered and torn. The butterfly ends its short life, pitching into a tangle of weeds. The tiny heart stops, the legs curl, the wings sink.

Twenty feet away, the butterfly eggs hatch on the cassia plant. The hungry offspring of the two yellow butterflies begin their brief, gentle days among the sun-kissed flowers of earth.

Author's Note

The long-distance butterfly traveler in the story is a cloudless sulphur *(Phoebis sennae)*. You may see this pale yellow-winged butterfly if you live in the southern and eastern United States. The cloudless sulphur is not found in the extreme North.

Cloudless sulphurs wander widely and can migrate great distances. Some biologists believe when certain areas in the tropics become crowded with butterflies, some species of butterflies find other places to live. Overcrowding may force cloudless sulphurs to migrate from the tropics to northern regions where they can find food plants for their larvae.

From the rain forests of the Yucatan Peninsula, Central America, and Cuba, these butterflies fly to the southern and central United States. On occasion, some even stray as far north as New England, a distance of 2,000 miles. Other butterfly travelers include painted ladies, red admirals, and buckeyes. The monarch butterfly is the only species that has a birdlike migration, flying south in the fall and north in the spring. Cloudless sulphur adults may visit your garden if you grow red pentas, red impatiens, hibiscus, or daisies. Their caterpillars feed on the leaves of cassia plants, a family of yellow-flowering herbs that are necessary for the survival of the cloudless sulphur.

How could an insect that weighs half a gram — a lot less than a dime — fly 2,000 miles? This fragile insect, buffeted by winds, attacked by predators, slashed by rain, must find food and shelter on its arduous journey. But every year the cloudless sulphur, half the size of a CD, flies great distances from its tropical home. There are many amazing migrating animals on Earth — hummingbirds, sea turtles, whales. Yet, as a naturalist, I'm in awe of a long-distance traveler that sips only flower nectar for energy and pumps its paper-thin wings through miles and miles of airspace.